Rotary
Park City

Presents this book in honor of our speaker this

6ᵗʰ day of *October* , 20 20 .

Speech Title: *Intermountain Therapy Animals*

Speaker: _____

Speaker: *Kathy Klotz*

Speaker: *+ 6 dogs!*

BOOMER at your Service

Vanessa Keel &
Adriana Hernández Bergstrom

Clear Fork / Spork Publishing

Graduation Day at Pupperdine Academy was finally here!

Boomer could hardly wait to meet his new family. He listened for his name to be called, when...

Oh, no.
Boomer did not like bees.

Ahhh!
He jumped.

Oops!
He bounced.

Yikes!
He bumped.

Everyone laughed and teased Boomer for being afraid of a little bee.

Who'd want a scaredy-cat for a service dog? he thought.

Embarrassed, Boomer ran away as fast as he could.

How would he ever find a family to serve now?

Just then, a truck roared by heading toward an old man carrying groceries.

Boomer darted into the road and pushed the man to safety.

But instead of being grateful, the old man
yelled at Boomer for pouncing on him.

Boomer whimpered and walked away.

As he entered the park, Boomer spotted a girl plucking a flower.

"He loves me, he loves me not... he loves me! yes!"

The girl skipped away.

She forgot her flower! Boomer gathered the pretty petals and chased after her.

She must be allergic to dogs, he thought.

Time to keep looking.

Then, Boomer heard cheers and a loud
CRACK! in the distance.

He saw a ball soaring through the sky.

This was his chance.

Boomer caught the ball and raced back
to return it to a boy.

YOU'RE OUTTA HERE!

shouted a man.

Boos echoed from the crowd.

This was the most hurtful
rejection of all.

Boomer wondered if he would
ever find his forever home.

It was not looking good.

But then, Boomer heard something.
Was that a cry for help?

A kitten popped up from behind a rose bush.
"Well, hello there," Boomer said. "Are you lost?"

The kitten purred and rubbed her furry tail on Boomer.
"Hey, that tickles," he giggled.

Excited to help his new friend, Boomer took the kitten in search of her owner.

He looked all over the park until he heard...

here kitty kitty!

here kitty kitty!

"Kitty, where have you been? I worried all night."
The girl hugged her kitten.
Boomer sighed. *If only someone loved me that much.*

The girl read Boomer's tag. "Hi, Boomer. I'm Cecilia.

Thank you for bringing Kitty back. You're my hero!"
She planted a wet kiss right on Boomer's nose.

kisses were way better than bees!

"Would you like to come home with us?" she asked.
"We've been looking for someone just like you."
"Ruff," barked Boomer, wildly wagging his tail.

Boomer loved his new family.

He helped Mom carry
groceries from the car.

He picked flowers with
Kitty and Cecilia.

He played fetch with Dad.

But Boomer's favorite time of all was when he visited the Children's Hospital with Cecilia.

It turned out, Boomer made a perfect therapy dog because he was so great at making all the children laugh.

~Author's Note~

Service Dogs

Did you know service dogs are real life superheroes? With extraordinary powers, they can sense trouble before it happens, guide people who are blind, and help assist those who are hearing impaired. Service dogs can detect a spike or drop in sugar in a person with diabetes, calm a child with autism, and even warn someone who is about to have a seizure.

Like Boomer, not all dogs can be service dogs. There are certain traits a dog must have in order to become a certified service dog. Some dogs like Boomer, are much better at being trained therapy dogs giving special love and comfort to people who need it.

A Child's Guide: The Do's & Don'ts of Service Dogs (A message from Janice Wolfe, Canine Expert & Founder of Merlin's KIDS)

Service dogs wear special vests when they're on duty. But not all service dogs wear vests. That can make things confusing. If you see a dog in a place like a restaurant, the mall, a store, or an airplane, he is most likely a service dog. However, you can never be too sure.

Follow these safety rules whenever you see a dog:

Do
- Always ask permission to pet any dog
- Always give the owner and dog space
- Always use a calm voice

Don't
- Sneak up on or talk to a dog on duty
- Distract the dog from his work
- Approach a dog you don't know without an adult present

How Can You Help?

There are a variety of organizations that help train service dogs. One of my favorites is Merlin's KIDS, a non-profit organization dedicated to providing individually trained service dogs to those in need. They rescue dogs from shelters, train them, and give them a very meaningful purpose. These special dogs help transform children's lives by being lifelong friends, committed to making their companion's lives easier.

There are a variety of ways you can help Merlin's KIDS continue their mission.

Please visit www.merlinskids.org/donate to learn how you can support this incredible organization.

For coloring pages, curriculum guides, and other goodies, please visit: www.vanessakeel.com

To my amazing husband and darling son. You are my home.
I'm so glad I found you.
- V. K.

For all the dogs I've ever loved.
- A.H.B.

Vanessa Keel's love for dogs started at a young age. Pretending to be one at her parent's dinner parties eventually led to a puppy of her own. Vanessa spent her career creating award-winning advertising campaigns. Working at The Walt Disney Company is the time she cherishes most. Now, she has her own characters with their own stories that she hopes will bring joy to children everywhere. Vanessa lives in New Jersey with her husband and baby boy. She's currently negotiating with her husband to get a furry friend for their family. Wish her luck! To learn more, please visit www.vanessakeel.com

Adriana Hernández Bergstrom is a Cuban-American illustrator from Miami. When she's not painting kawaii critters, teaching, or petting puppies (with permission!), she's illustrating from her studio. Her work can be seen at adriprints.com

Boomer At Your Service
Text copyright © 2019 by Vanessa Keel · Illustrations copyright © 2019 by Adriana Bergstrom
Edited and Art Directed by Mira Reisberg www.childrensbookacademy.com

Summary: When disaster strikes at Boomer's Service Dog Graduation Day, he sets off to find a family on his own. Catastrophe after calamity leave him feeling hopeless until a furry feline changes his fate forever. Boomer discovers friendship, his happily-ever-after home, and his special purpose in life.

Clear Fork Publishing P.O. Box 870 102 S. Swenson Stamford, TX 79553 · (325)773-5550
www.clearforkpublishing.com Printed and Bound in the United States of America.

ISBN - 978-1-950169-20-7